MAYBE...

CHRIS HAUGHTON

"For the things we have to learn
before we can do, we learn by doing"
Aristotle

For May, Joanna and Cuan

First published 2021 by Walker Books Ltd
87 Vauxhall Walk, London SE11 5HJ
This edition published 2022
10 9 8 7 6 5 4 3 2 1
© 2021 Chris Haughton
The right of Chris Haughton to be identified as
the author and illustrator of this work has been asserted
by him in accordance with the Copyright, Designs and
Patents Act 1988
This book has been typeset in SHH
Printed in China

British Library Cataloguing in Publication Data:
a catalogue record for this book is available
from the British Library
Published by arrangement with Debbie Bibo Agency
ISBN 978-1-5295-0398-2
www.walker.co.uk   chrishaughton.com

WALKER BOOKS
AND SUBSIDIARIES
LONDON · BOSTON · SYDNEY · AUCKLAND

Ok, monkeys! I'm off.
Now remember...

Whatever you do,
do NOT go down to the mango tree.
There are tigers down there.

It's a pity
we can't go
down to the
mango tree.

Hmm ...
maybe ...

Any tigers here?
No!

Any tigers there?
No!

No tigers anywhere!
It's safe.

Down,
down,
down,

to
the
trees
below.

And LOOK!

So many
mangos!

Oh...
There's one
within reach
just over
there.

maybe we could just
get that little one.
We'd keep a close look out.
That'd be ok, right?

Quick as
a flash!

Down,
grab the
mango,
and climb
back up.

I wish we had another
one though...

Down,
down,
down,

all the way down
to the GROUND.

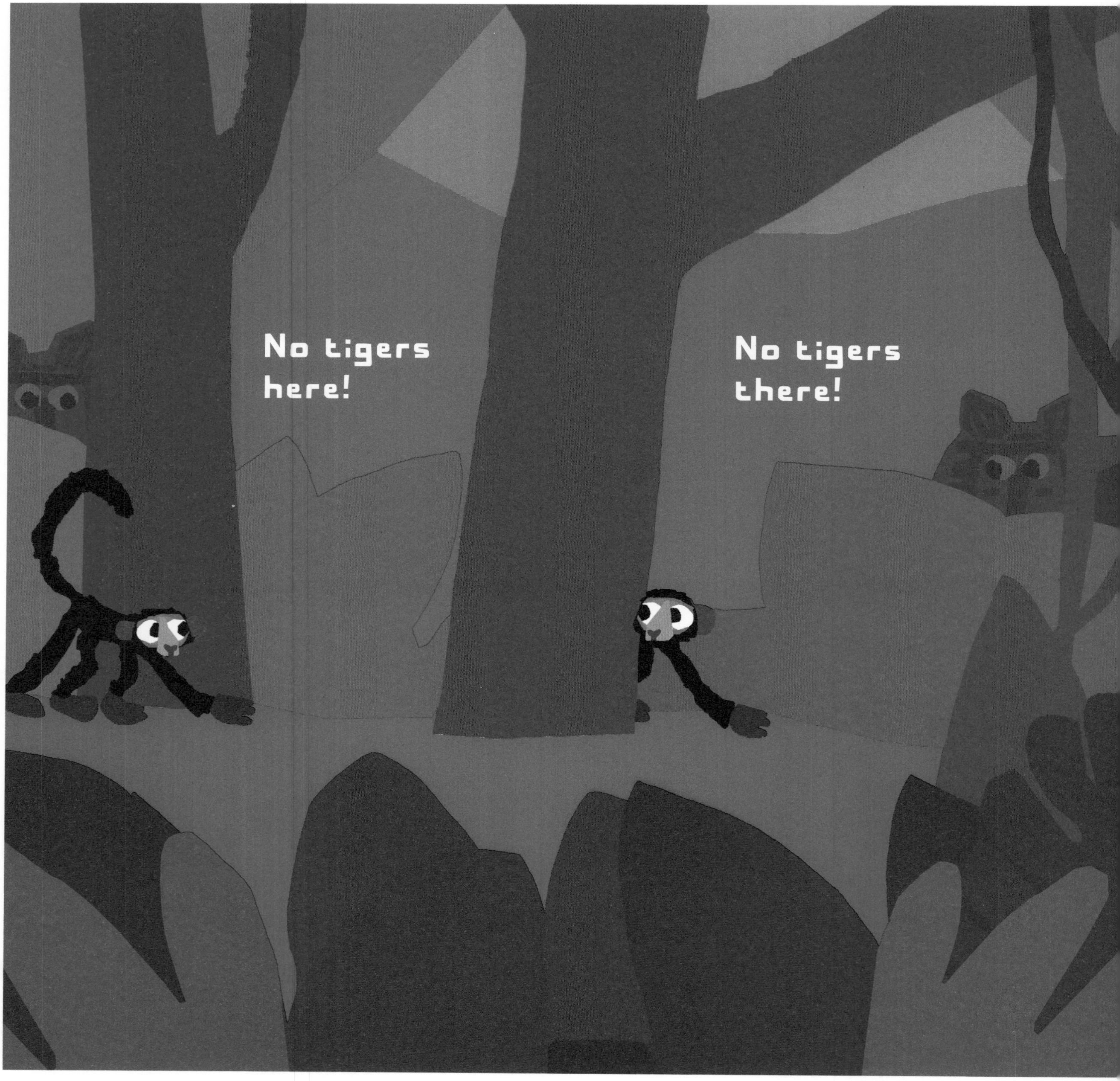

No tigers here!

No tigers there!

No tigers
anywhere!

And LOOK!
ALL the mangos.

Wait ...
did I hear
something?

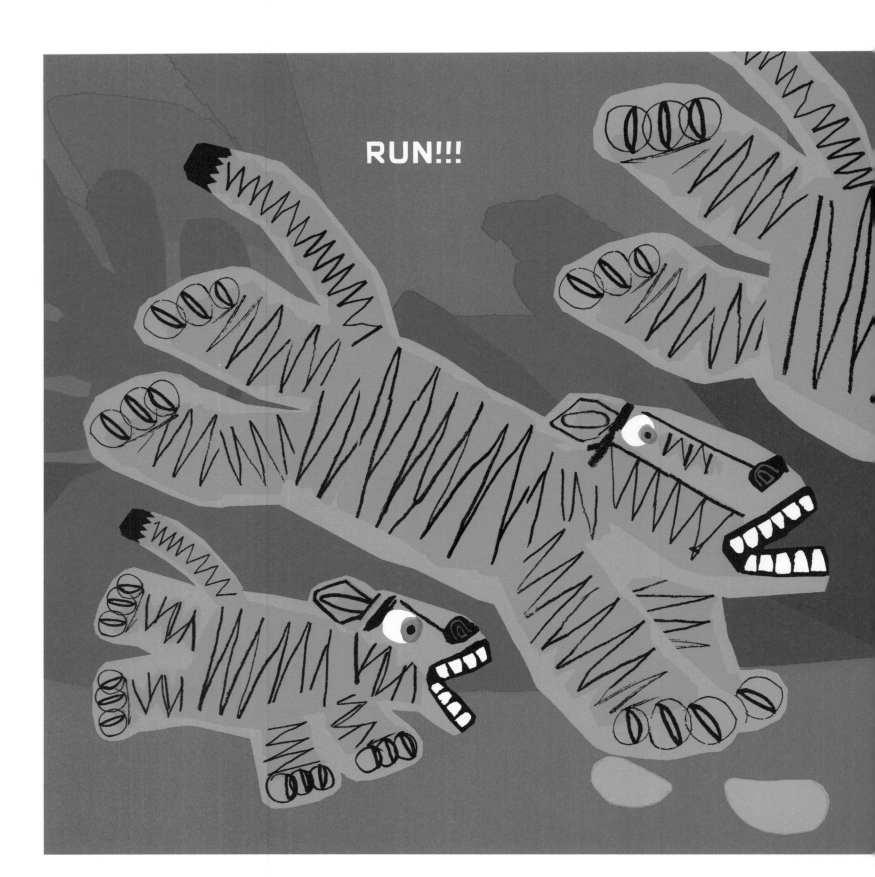

Oh! It's lucky you're
all the way up here.
Did you see?

There are tigers
everywhere down there.

Well, we'll have to stay up here now. We can't go anywhere. Not even to the bananas.

There are bananas?

maybe...